4/05
008

✓

Petronella

by JAY WILLIAMS

with pictures by FRISO HENSTRA

Parents' Magazine Press / New York

Other books by Jay Williams

The Cookie Tree
The King with Six Friends
The Practical Princess
A Present from a Bird
School for Sillies
Seven at One Blow
The Silver Whistle
Stupid Marco
The Youngest Captain

Text copyright © 1973 by Jay Williams
Illustrations copyright © 1973 by Friso Henstra
All rights reserved. Printed in the United States of America

Library of Congress Cataloging in Publication Data
Williams, Jay, 1914-
  Petronella.
  SUMMARY: Determined not to be outdone by her brothers
in seeking a fortune in the world, a young princess sets
out to find a prince to rescue.
  [1. Fairy tales]   I. Henstra, Friso, illus.
II. Title.
PZ8.W6696Pe   398.2'1 [E]   72-6066
ISBN 0-8193-0636-3   ISBN 0-8193-0637-1 (lib. ed.)

In the kingdom of Skyclear Mountain, three princes were always born to the king and queen. The oldest prince was always called Michael, the middle prince was always called George, and the youngest was always called Peter. When they were grown, they always went out to seek their fortunes. What happened to the oldest prince and the middle prince no one ever knew. But the youngest prince always rescued a princess, brought her home, and in time ruled over the kingdom. That was the way it had always been. And so far as anyone knew, that was the way it would always be.

Until now.

Now was the time of King Peter the twenty-sixth and Queen Blossom. An oldest prince was born, and a middle prince. But the youngest prince turned out to be a girl.

"Well," said the king gloomily, "we can't call her Peter. We'll have to call her Petronella. And what's to be done about it, I'm sure I don't know."

There was nothing to be done. The years passed, and the time came for the princes to go out and seek their fortunes. Michael and George said good-bye to the king and queen and mounted their horses. Then out came Petronella. She was dressed in traveling clothes, with her bag packed and a sword by her side.

"If you think," she said, "that I'm going to sit at home, you are mistaken. I'm going to seek my fortune, too."

"Impossible!" said the king.

"What will people say?" cried the queen.

"Look," said Prince Michael, "be reasonable, Pet. Stay home. Sooner or later a prince will turn up here."

Petronella smiled. She was a tall, handsome girl with flaming red hair, and when she smiled in that particular way it meant she was trying to keep her temper.

"I'm going with you," she said. "I'll find a prince if I have to rescue one from something myself. And that's that."

The grooms brought out her horse, she said good-bye to her parents, and away she went behind her two brothers.

They traveled into the flatlands below Skyclear Mountain. After many days, they entered a great dark forest. They came to a place where the road divided into three, and there at the fork sat a little, wrinkled old man covered with dust and spiderwebs.

Prince Michael said haughtily, "Where do these roads go, old man?"

"The road on the right goes to the city of Gratz," the man replied. "The road in the center goes to the castle of Blitz. The road on the left goes to the house of Albion the enchanter. And that's one."

"What do you mean by 'And that's one'?" asked Prince George.

"I mean," said the old man, "that I am forced to sit on this spot without stirring, and that I must answer one question from each person who passes by. And that's two."

Petronella's kind heart was touched. "Is there anything I can do to help you?" she asked.

The old man sprang to his feet. The dust fell from him in clouds.

"You have already done so," he said. "For that question is the one which releases me. I have sat here for sixty-two years waiting for someone to ask me that." He snapped his fingers with joy. "In return, I will tell you anything you wish to know."

"Where can I find a prince?" Petronella said promptly.

"There is one in the house of Albion the enchanter," the old man answered.

"Ah," said Petronella, "then that is where I am going."

"In that case I will leave you," said her oldest brother. "For I am going to the castle of Blitz to see if I can find my fortune there."

"Good luck," said Prince George. "For I am going to the city of Gratz. I have a feeling my fortune is there."

They embraced her and rode away.

Petronella looked thoughtfully at the old man, who was combing spiderwebs and dust out of his beard. "May I ask you something else?" she said.

"Of course. Anything."

"Suppose I wanted to rescue that prince from the enchanter. How would I go about it? I haven't any experience in such things, you see."

The old man chewed a piece of his beard. "I do not know everything," he said, after a moment. "I know that there are three magical secrets which, if you can get them from him, will help you."

"How can I get them?" asked Petronella.

"Offer to work for him. He will set you three tasks, and if you can do them you may demand a reward for each. You must ask him for a comb for your hair, a mirror to look into, and a ring for your finger."

"And then?"

"I do not know. I only know that when you rescue the prince, you can use these things to escape from the enchanter."

"It doesn't sound easy," sighed Petronella.

"Nothing we really want is easy," said the old man. "Look at me—I have wanted my freedom, and I've had to wait sixty-two years for it."

Petronella said good-bye to him. She mounted her horse and galloped along the third road.

It ended at a low, rambling house with a red roof. It was a comfortable-looking house, surrounded by gardens and stables and trees heavy with fruit.

On the lawn, in an armchair, sat a handsome young man with his eyes closed and his face turned to the sky.

Petronella tied her horse to the gate and walked across the lawn.

"Is this the house of Albion the enchanter?" she said.

The young man blinked up at her in surprise.

"I think so," he said. "Yes, I'm sure it is."

"And who are you?"

The young men yawned and stretched. "I am Prince Ferdinand of Firebright," he replied. "Would you mind stepping aside? I'm trying to get a suntan and you're standing in the way."

Petronella snorted. "You don't sound like much of a prince," she said.

"That's funny," said the young man, closing his eyes. "That's what my father always says."

At that moment the door of the house opened. Out came a man dressed all in black and silver. He was tall and thin, and as sinister as a cloud full of thunder. His face was stern, but full of wisdom. Petronella knew at once that he must be the enchanter.

He bowed to her politely. "What can I do for you?"

"I wish to work for you," said Petronella boldly.

Albion nodded. "I cannot refuse you," he said. "But I warn you, it will be dangerous. Tonight I will give you a task. If you do it, I will reward you. If you fail, you must die."

Petronella glanced at the prince and sighed. "If I must, I must," she said. "Very well."

That evening they all had dinner together in the enchanter's cozy kitchen. Then Albion took Petronella out to a stone building and unbolted its door. Inside were seven huge black dogs.

"You must watch my hounds all night," said he.

Petronella went in, and Albion closed and locked the door.

At once the hounds began to snarl and bark. They showed their teeth at her. But Petronella was a real princess. She plucked up her courage. Instead of backing away, she went toward the dogs. She began to speak to them in a quiet voice. They stopped snarling and sniffed at her. She patted their heads.

"I see what it is," she said. "You are lonely here. I will keep you company."

And so all night long, she sat on the floor and talked to the hounds and stroked them. They lay close to her, panting.

In the morning Albion came and let her out. "Ah," said he, "I see that you are brave. If you had run from the dogs, they would have torn you to pieces. Now you may ask for what you want."

"I want a comb for my hair," said Petronella.

The enchanter gave her a comb carved from a piece of black wood.

Prince Ferdinand was sunning himself and working at a crossword puzzle. Petronella said to him in a low voice, "I am doing this for you."

"That's nice," said the prince. "What's 'selfish' in nine letters?"

"You are," snapped Petronella. She went to the enchanter. "I will work for you once more," she said.

That night Albion led her to a stable. Inside were seven huge horses.

"Tonight," he said, "you must watch my steeds."

He went out and locked the door. At once the horses began to rear and neigh. They pawed at her with their iron hoofs.

But Petronella was a real princess. She looked closely at them and saw that their coats were rough and their manes and tails full of burrs.

"I see what it is," she said. "You are hungry and dirty."

She brought them as much hay as they could eat, and began to brush them. All night long she fed them and groomed them, and they stood quietly in their stalls.

In the morning Albion let her out. "You are as kind as you are brave," said he. "If you had run from them, they would have trampled you under their hoofs. What will you have as a reward?"

"I want a mirror to look into," said Petronella.

The enchanter gave her a mirror made of gray silver.

She looked across the lawn at Prince Ferdinand. He was doing setting-up exercises. He was certainly handsome. She said to the enchanter, "I will work for you once more."

That night Albion led her to a loft above the stables. There, on perches, were seven great hawks.

"Tonight," said he, "you must watch my falcons."

As soon as Petronella was locked in, the hawks began to beat their wings and scream at her.

Petronella laughed. "That is not how birds sing," she said. "Listen."

She began to sing in a sweet voice. The hawks fell silent. All night long she sang to them, and they sat like feathered statues on their perches, listening.

In the morning Albion said, "You are as talented as you are kind and brave. If you had run from them, they would have pecked and clawed you without mercy. What do you want now?"

"I want a ring for my finger," said Petronella.

The enchanter gave her a ring made from a single diamond.

All that day and all that night Petronella slept, for she was very tired. But early the next morning, she crept into Prince Ferdinand's room. He was sound asleep, wearing purple pajamas.

"Wake up," whispered Petronella. "I am going to rescue you."

Ferdinand awoke and stared sleepily at her. "What time is it?"

"Never mind that," said Petronella. "Come on!"

"But I'm sleepy," Ferdinand objected. "And it's so pleasant here."

Petronella shook her head. "You're not much of a prince," she said grimly. "But you're the best I can do."

She grabbed him by the wrist and dragged him out of bed. She hauled him down the stairs. His horse and hers were in a separate stable, and she saddled them quickly. She gave the prince a shove, and he mounted. She jumped on her own horse, seized the prince's reins, and away they went like the wind.

They had not gone far when they heard a tremendous thumping. Petronella looked back. A dark cloud rose behind them, and beneath it she saw the enchanter. He was running with great strides, faster than the horses could go.

Petronella desperately pulled out the comb. "The old man said this would help me!" she said. And because she didn't know what else to do with it, she threw the comb on the ground.

At once a forest rose up. The trees were so thick that no one could get between them.

Away went Petronella and the prince. But the enchanter turned himself into an ax and began to chop. Right and left he chopped, flashing, and the trees fell before him.

Soon he was through the wood, and once again Petronella heard his footsteps thumping behind.

She reined in the horses. She took out the mirror and threw it on the ground. At once a wide lake spread out behind them, gray and glittering.

Off they went again. But the enchanter sprang into the water, turning himself into a salmon as he did so. He swam across the lake and leaped out of the water on to the other bank. Petronella heard him coming—*thump! thump!*—behind them again.

This time she threw down the ring. It didn't turn into anything, but lay shining on the ground.

The enchanter came running up. And as he jumped over the ring, it opened wide and then snapped up around him. It held his arms tight to his body, in a magical grip from which he could not escape.

"Well," said Prince Ferdinand, "that's the end of him."

Petronella looked at him in annoyance. Then she looked at the enchanter, held fast in the ring.

"Bother!" she said. "I can't just leave him here. He'll starve to death."

She got off her horse and went up to him. "If I release you," she said, "will you promise to let the prince go free?"

Albion stared at her in astonishment. "Let him go free?" he said. "What are you talking about? I'm glad to get rid of him."

It was Petronella's turn to look surprised. "I don't understand," she said. "Weren't you holding him prisoner?"

"Certainly not," said Albion. "He came to visit me for a weekend. At the end of it, he said, 'It's so pleasant here, do you mind if I stay on for another day or two?' I'm very polite and I said, 'Of course.' He stayed on, and on, and on. I didn't like to be rude to a guest and I couldn't just kick him out. I don't know what I'd have done if you hadn't dragged him away."

"But then—" said Petronella, "but then—why did you come running after him this way?"

"I wasn't chasing him," said the enchanter. "I was chasing *you*. You are just the girl I've been looking for. You are brave and kind and talented, and beautiful as well."

"Oh," said Petronella.

"I see," she said.

"Hmm," said she. "How do I get this ring off you?"

"Give me a kiss."

She did so. The ring vanished from around Albion and reappeared on Petronella's finger.

"I don't know what my parents will say when I come home with you instead of a prince," she said.

"Let's go and find out, shall we?" said the enchanter cheerfully.

He mounted one horse and Petronella the other. And off they trotted, side by side, leaving Prince Ferdinand of Firebright to walk home as best he could.